JESSICA SOUHAMI studied at the Central School of Art and Design. In 1980 she set up a travelling puppet company using colourful shadow puppets with music and a storyteller. She is internationally acclaimed for her picture-book folktale retellings, bringing some of the world's great stories to a young audience. Her recent books for Frances Lincoln include *Sausages*, *Piglet's Picnic*, *The Sticky Doll Trap* and *King Pom and the Fox*. Jessica lives in north London.

70001614065 X

JANETTA OTTER-BARRY BOOKS

Text and illustrations copyright © Jessica Souhami 2012
First published in Great Britain in 2012 and in the USA in 2013 by
Frances Lincoln Children's Books,
74-77 White Lion Street, London N1 9PF
www.franceslincoln.com

First paperback published in 2013

A catalogue record for this book is available from the British Library.

ISBN 978-1-84780-498-3

Illustrated with collage of Ingres papers hand-painted with watercolour inks and graphite pencil

Set in MinisterLT

Printed in China

1 3 5 7 9 8 6 4 2

FOXY!

Jessica Souhami

F

FRANCES LINCOLN
CHILDREN'S BOOKS

One day Foxy caught a bee.

He put it in his sack and he went on his travels.

He travelled and he travelled and he travelled until...

he met a woman who had a fine rooster.

"Good day," he said. "Will you look after
my sack while I go to Squintum's house?"
"Certainly," said the woman.
"Thank you," said Foxy. "But whatever you do,

DON'T LOOK IN THE SACK!"

And off he went.

But the woman just had to have a little peep.
She opened the sack just the tiniest bit –

and...

OUT flew the bee,

and her rooster chased it

and chased it

and chased it away!

Just then Foxy came back and he saw the empty sack.

"Where's my bee?" he asked.

"Gone," whispered the woman.

"Very well," said Foxy. "I must take your rooster."

So he put the rooster in his sack and he went on his travels.

And he travelled and he travelled and he travelled

until...

he met a man who had a fat pig.

"Good day," he said. "Will you look after
my sack while I go to Squintum's house?"
"Gladly," said the man.
"Thank you," said Foxy. "But whatever you do,

DON'T LOOK IN THE SACK!"

And off he went.

But the man just had to have a little peep.
He opened the sack just the teensiest bit –

and…

OUT flew the rooster,

and his pig chased it

and chased it

and chased it away!

Just then Foxy came back and he saw the empty sack.
"Where's my rooster?" he asked.
"Gone," sighed the man.
"Very well," said Foxy. "I must take your pig."

So he put the pig in his sack and he went on his travels.

And he travelled and he travelled and he travelled

until...

he met a little boy.

"Good day," he said. "Will you look after
my sack while I go to Squintum's house?"
"Yes, Sir!" said the little boy.
"Thank you," said Foxy. "But whatever you do,

DON'T LOOK IN THE SACK!"

And off he went.

But the boy just had to have a little peep.
He opened the sack just the weensiest bit –

and...

OUT jumped the pig,

and the little boy chased it

and chased it

and chased it away!

Just then Foxy came back and he saw the empty sack.
"Where's my pig?" he asked.
The little boy just shrugged.
"Very well," said Foxy.
"I must take YOU!"

So he put the little boy in his sack and he went on his travels.

And he travelled and he travelled and he travelled

until…

he met a woman baking cakes.

"Good day," he said. "Will you look after
my sack while I go to Squintum's house?"
"By all means," said the woman.
"Thank you," said Foxy. "But whatever you do,

DON'T LOOK IN THE SACK!"

And off he went.

Now, the woman didn't look in the sack.

Her cakes were ready and she took them out of the oven. My, but they smelled good to the little boy in the bag.

He was HUNGRY.

"Please, Ma'am," he called out. "May I have some cake?"

"Goodness me!" cried the woman.
"A child in the sack.
WICKED OLD FOXY!"

She opened the sack
and lifted the boy out.

And she put her big dog in the sack instead.
Then she tied the sack tight.

Just then Foxy came back.
He saw that his sack was shut,
so he picked it up
and went on his travels.

And he travelled and he travelled and he travelled

until...

he came to some woods.
"I'm hungry," he said.
"I think I'll eat that little boy now."
So he opened the sack

and...

OUT JUMPED THE BIG DOG

AND IT CHASED HIM

AND IT CHASED HIM AND IT CHASED HIM AWAY.

And Foxy was never seen again!

And that is the end of this story.